STANLEY in the DARK

M. Christina Butler
illustrated by
Meg Rutherford

BARRON'S

New York · Toronto

There was nothing Stanley Mouse liked better
than cheese.
He dreamed about it every time he went
to sleep.
Red cheese; green cheese; cheese with holes;
hard yellow cheese and soft cream cheese.
Stanley loved any kind of cheese.

One night, when you were fast asleep,
Stanley looked about.
He couldn't believe his eyes.
There in front of him was the roundest,
juiciest, creamiest cheese he had
ever seen – stuck in a tree.
He couldn't wait to sink his teeth into it.

With great leaps and jumps he scampered
across the grass.
But wait.

Stanley was not alone in the meadow.
"W-who's there?" he squeaked in his
biggest and bravest voice.

"Only us," replied Mother Porcupine.
"My babies and I are looking for our supper."
"Come and have some cheese, then," said Stanley.
"Cheese?" asked Mother Porcupine. "What cheese?"

"That cheese," said Stanley.

"The cheese that is stuck in the tree."

"Oh, *that* cheese," said Mother Porcupine and she giggled as she and her babies ran off.

All the more for me, thought Stanley
as he ran towards the tree.

But Stanley was not alone near the tree.
"W-who's there?" he squeaked in his
biggest and bravest voice.

"Only me," replied Fox, creeping nearer.
"What is a tiny mouse like you doing so far
from his mousehole?"
"I've come for some cheese," said Stanley.
"Cheese?" asked Fox. "What cheese?"
"The cheese that is stuck in this tree,"
said Stanley.
"Oh, *that* cheese," sneered Fox.

Then suddenly he pounced.
But Stanley, as quick as a flash, ran up
the tree trunk.

Higher and higher he climbed, up and up.
But where was the cheese?
He looked here and sniffed there.
He couldn't find it anywhere.

Stanley was not alone in the tree.
"W-who's there?" he cried in his
biggest and bravest voice.

"Only me," said Owl, hopping closer.
"Have you seen a big, yellow cheese?" asked
Stanley. "It was stuck in this tree."

"Do you mean," said Owl, putting out two talons,
"*that* cheese over there?"
"Yes, that's it!" said Stanley, as he dived
off the branch for the cheese . . .

. . . and fell
     down,
          down,
               down . . .

. . . into the reeds near the pond.

When Stanley opened his eyes, he couldn't
believe what he saw. There was the cheese,
right in front of his nose.

With a squeak of delight,
he jumped out of the reeds and
fell into the pond.

Poor Stanley! How he gasped and gulped,
coughed and spluttered.
Then he began to swim with all his might.

At last he reached the bank,
pulled himself out of the water,
and there he lay, exhausted.
But Stanley was not alone on the bank.

"Is that a mouse I see?" said Cat,
her eyes wide and bright.
"I am in luck tonight."
The tall grasses trembled as she
prepared to pounce.

But they were not alone beside the pond.
"Who's there?" hissed Cat in her
biggest and loudest voice.

"Me!" barked Dog, bouncing through the
bushes and chasing Cat out of the grass,
away across the field.

Now Stanley WAS alone on the bank,
except for something in the grass.
After a while, the smell of it made him
sit up and rub his eyes.
Someone had been picnicking near the pond
that day and had left behind a piece
of cheese!
Stanley sniffed around until he found it.

He picked it up as fast as he could and
with great leaps and jumps
he scampered back across the meadow.

As night became day, Stanley sat
and ate his supper.

The next time Stanley
went to sleep,
he dreamed about the
cheese in the tree,
of how he had caught it and
brought it home . . .

The biggest cheese he had ever seen.
The cheese that was stuck in a tree!